LAMPLAND

to the Noom

Launch pad

the Seventh Sea

Sweet Factory

Rainbow Meadows

Techno Town

Castle Kinghold

City of Ancients

to Crossbone Island

Mermaid Reef

Red Dragon Hills

Fairy Forest

Land of the Giants

Monster Mountain

Mr Mistry, Genie Street's postman, gives Tom and Daisy a special parcel which sends them on each new adventure!

GENIE STREET

Mr Slater
GLADIATOR

Contents

Chapter One
The Wrong Way Round

The magic street lamp
wasn't working.

'I don't understand it!' said
Tom. He looked at his hand.
He looked at the lamp post.
'I'm *sure* I rubbed it the
right way.'

'Have another go!' said his
sister, Daisy.

So Tom tried again.

'*Once up… once down…*'
muttered Tom, concentrating.
'*Then three times round
and round…*'

Daisy watched eagerly.
But still nothing happened.

Usually, if you rubbed the
street lamp like this, it lit up.
Its magic purple light showed
the way to another world.

But today there wasn't even
the faintest sparkle.

'Perhaps it's broken,' said Tom.

'We might *never* get back to Lampland!' said Daisy sadly.

'Now, now!' said a third voice. 'Let's not get our tails in a twist!'

The children looked down. A black and white cat was looking back up at them.

'Hi, Jinx!' cried Tom.

'It's just your *round-and-rounds*,' purred the cat. 'You're doing them in the wrong direction, that's all.'

'Remember when I first showed you?' said Jinx. 'I went *this* way...'

He looped round Tom's legs in a clockwise direction.

'Of course!' said Tom. 'I didn't think! I'll do it again!'

This time, the street lamp blazed into life. A ball of purple light burst from its top and shot along the street.

Chapter Two

A Passage to Where?

'Did you see?' cried Daisy.
'It hit Mr Slater's house!'

Mr Slater lived at number 5.
He worked at a bank in the
city. He walked past Tom
and Daisy's house early
every morning, on his way
to catch his train.

'Although I haven't seen
him lately,' said Tom.

The children expected to find Mr Slater's front door glowing purple. But it wasn't.

'Are you *sure* this is where the light hit?' asked Tom.

Before Daisy could answer, there was a sudden screech of brakes and a strong smell of fireworks. The children heard a familiar voice, right behind them.

'Hullo! Hullo!'

19

It was Mr Mistry, the Genie Street postman.

'Special Delivery for Mr Slater!' he beamed. He handed a tiny parcel to Daisy.

'Wow!' cried Tom, staring. 'Where did you get that bike, Mr Mistry? Is it *rocket*-powered?'

With a wink, Mr Mistry rang his bell. There was a loud bang and a billow of purple smoke.

When it cleared, the children were alone.

21

'Let's deliver this parcel!' said Daisy. She turned – and gasped. 'Look, Tom!'

Mr Slater's house had a side passage. Its iron gate was glowing faintly purple.

'It's opening!' cried Tom.

The gate rose slowly. The passage beyond swirled with purple mist.

Jinx strolled up. Without a word, he set off along the misty passage. Tom and Daisy hurried after him.

23

Chapter Three
Lion on the Loose

After only a few strides, Tom and Daisy stepped out of the mist – into the centre of a large, circular arena.

Tiers of seating, built of stone, rose up all around them. They were packed with people. The crowd welcomed the children with a loud cheer.

'It's an amphitheatre,' purred Jinx.

'A *what*?' said Tom.

'It's where gladiators fight!' said Daisy. 'Like in Ancient Rome!'

'Exactly,' said Jinx. 'But we're not in Rome. We're in the City of Ancients, the oldest city in Lampland.'

Tom wasn't really listening. He was too busy staring at the huge, hungry-looking lion that was pacing around the arena.

The lion prowled towards
them, growling. Tom and
Daisy froze with fear.

'Do something, Jinx!'
squeaked Tom. 'You can
speak cat language! Tell
it we taste nasty!'

'I'm terribly sorry,' purred
Jinx. 'I'm afraid I don't
speak Big Cat. Siamese, yes.
Lionish, no.'

The lion got ready to pounce.
Daisy screamed.

Suddenly, a man in a tunic and helmet dashed into the arena. He was carrying a spear and a net. He rushed at the lion bravely.

The lion roared. It lashed out at the man with a deadly paw.

Again and again, the man dodged the lion's sharp claws. Then, with perfect timing, he flung his net.

The net dropped over the lion. It tried to shake it off, snarling. But the lion only got more tangled and finally fell over. In the end, the lion gave up struggling and sat still.

The crowd cheered and clapped – all except two men. They sat in a grand balcony, wearing fine robes. Both men were scowling.

'That's the emperor and his son,' purred Jinx. '*Very* grumpy.'

The man in the arena walked over to the children. He took off his helmet.

'Mr Slater!' cried Tom.

'You were brilliant!' said Daisy. 'Thanks for saving us!'

Mr Slater gave a half-smile. 'I'm afraid we're not out of trouble *yet*,' he said.

Two guards were striding towards them, holding spears. They didn't look friendly.

Chapter Four
Down in the Dungeon

The guards took Mr Slater's
spear. They marched him,
Tom and Daisy across
the arena and along a
gloomy tunnel. It led to an
underground dungeon. The
guards shoved all three of them
into a barred cell. They locked
its door and marched off.

'What's going on, Mr Slater?' asked Tom. 'Why have they locked us up?'

'Emperor's orders, I'm afraid,' said Mr Slater. 'I'm a prisoner, you see. Until last week, I was a happy citizen of the City of Ancients. A free man. But things have changed. I'm a slave now.'

'It looks like we are, too!' said Daisy.

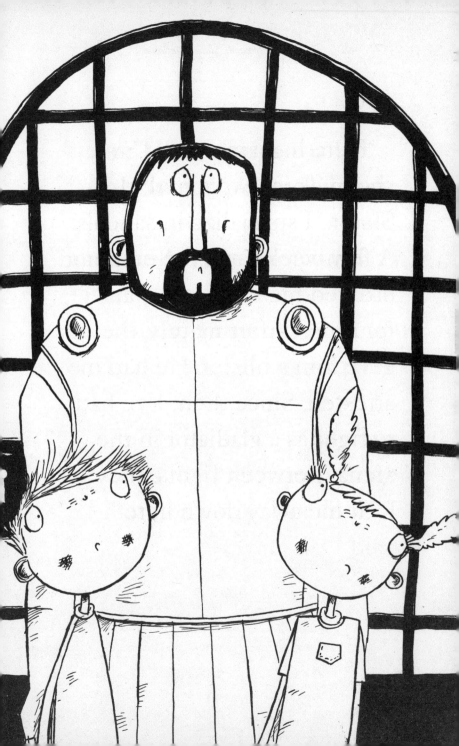

'Here in Lampland, I'm a shoemaker,' explained Mr Slater. 'I specialize in sandals. A few weeks ago, the emperor ordered me to make a pair for him. Unfortunately, they gave him a blister. He had me arrested. Since then, I've had to fight as a gladiator in the arena. Between fights, they lock me away down here.'

'That's awful!' said Daisy. 'We have to get you out!'

'And Brian, too,' said Mr Slater. 'I couldn't leave him behind.'

'Brian?' said Tom and Daisy together.

'The lion,' said Mr Slater. 'We've become great friends. Don't let all that roaring fool you. It's all part of our act. He's a big pussycat, really.'

'Right,' said Tom. 'If you say so.'

Chapter Five
The Key to the Problem

'Talking of pussycats,' said
Daisy, 'where's Jinx got to?'

'*Hurumf-arumf!*' mumbled
a voice outside the cell.

Jinx appeared, with a parcel
in his mouth. He let it fall
through the bars.

'I thought you might want
that,' he purred. 'You dropped
it back in the arena.'

'Of course!' cried Daisy.
'Mr Mistry's Special Delivery!'

Mr Slater unwrapped the parcel. He held up a large brass key. It had a solid, square end.

'That won't unlock anything!' groaned Tom.

'Try the door, Mr Slater!' urged Daisy.

As Mr Slater pushed the key into the lock, its end began to sparkle. It fitted perfectly. He turned it and the door swung open.

'I wish we could free everyone,' said Mr Slater. He looked sadly around the dungeon. 'But the guards have a different key for each slave's cell.'

'I wonder…' murmured Daisy. She took the brass key and hurried to another cell door. The end of the key sparkled and shifted shape again. It turned smoothly in the lock.

Soon every cell was unlocked.
Mr Slater even let Brian out
of his cage. The children were
rather scared – until Brian gave
them both a huge, wet lick.

Together, the freed slaves
crept silently to the dungeon's
exit. Two guards stood on duty.

'We'll distract them,' Tom
whispered to Daisy. 'It should
give everyone else a chance to
get away! Ready?'

Chapter Six
The Chase

Tom and Daisy burst out
of hiding and dashed past
the guards.

'Wooo-hooo! Can't catch us!'
teased Daisy.

The children sprinted off
down a passageway. Both guards
ran after them, yelling.

Mr Slater, Brian and the others
quickly made their escape.

Tom and Daisy kept running.
The guards were right behind
them. The children had no
idea where the passage led
– until they burst out into
daylight.

'Rats!' puffed Tom. 'We're…
back… in… the arena!'

Two horse-drawn chariots
stood nearby. It looked like
the next arena event was going
to be a chariot race.

'Come on!' cried Daisy. She ran over to the nearest chariot. Tom jumped in beside her. Daisy grabbed the reins and gave them a good tug. The horse set off at a trot.

Tom looked back anxiously to see where the guards were. They were climbing into the other chariot.

The crowd cheered. The race was on.

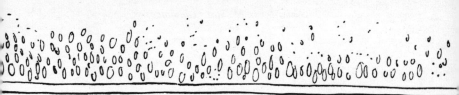

Daisy and Tom hung on for dear life as their horse began to gallop. Their chariot tore around the arena.

But the guards were gaining on them. On the third lap, their chariot pulled alongside the children's.

The driving guard made his horse swerve. The chariots smashed together. Daisy lost control.

'We're going to crash!' she cried.

Chapter Seven
Crashing Out

There was a gasp from the crowd as Tom and Daisy's chariot broke away from its horse. It swerved wildly, then headed straight for the stone wall of the amphitheatre.

'Arrrrghhhhhh!' screamed the children. The wall rushed towards them. They shut their eyes tightly.

Instead of a loud crash, the rush of air and the noise of the crowd suddenly stopped.

Tom and Daisy opened their eyes. They were back on Genie Street.

Mr Slater was closing his front door. He was dressed in his suit, ready for work.

'We all made it to freedom, thanks to you two!' he smiled. 'Even our four-legged friend.' He brushed a long golden hair from his suit and winked.

Mr Slater opened his briefcase. He took out two pairs of roman-style leather sandals.

'These are for you,' he told Tom and Daisy. 'A souvenir from the City of Ancients. Let's hope they don't give *you* blisters, hmm?' He winked again.

Tom and Daisy grinned. They thanked Mr Slater for the sandals, then hurried home to try them on…

GENIE STREET

Madame Zarr
CIRCUS STAR

Contents

Chapter One
Tracks in the Snow

A thick blanket of snow covered Genie Street.

'Doesn't it look perfect?' said Daisy, to her brother, Tom. 'I love being the first to walk in fresh snow!'

'We're not quite the first,' replied Tom. 'Look!'

A trail of small paw prints crossed the snowy road.

'They look like cat tracks,' said Tom. 'I bet Jinx made them.'

Jinx was their remarkable friend – a talking cat with a nose for adventure.

'Come on!' said Daisy. 'Let's see where he went!'

The paw prints led straight to the street lamp outside the Genie Street shops.

'We should have guessed!' laughed Tom.

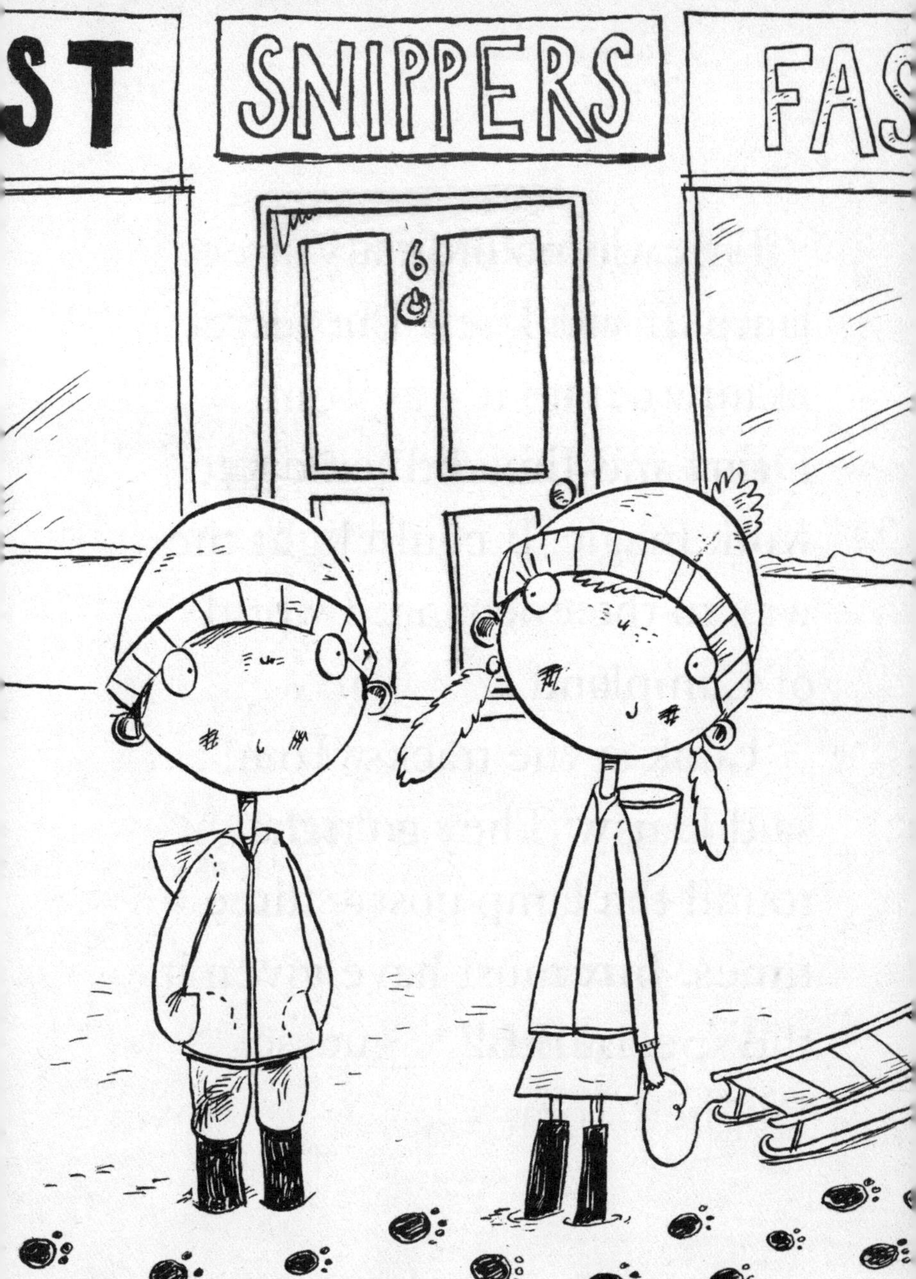
ST
SNIPPERS
FAS
6

This was no ordinary street lamp. If you knew the secret of how to rub it – as Tom, Daisy and Jinx did – it could work magic. It could light the way to the enchanted world of Lampland.

'Look at the tracks, Tom!' said Daisy. 'They go right round the lamp post – three times. Jinx must have given it the special rub!'

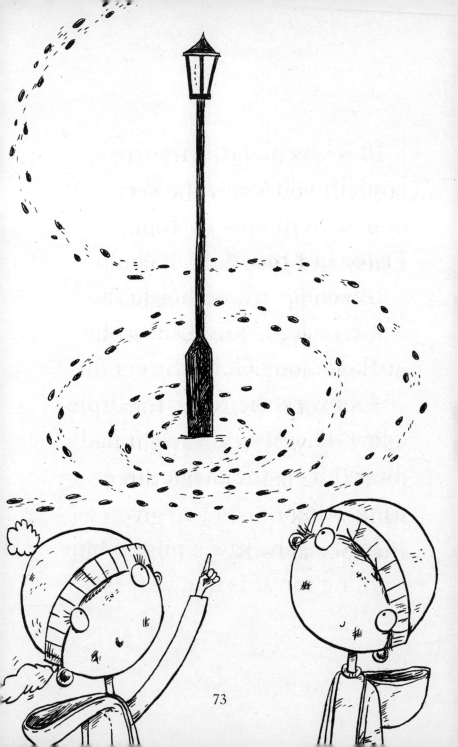

'It looks like it, doesn't it?' said Tom. '*Once up… once down… then three times round and round…*'

'I wonder whose house the lamp picked,' said Daisy. She looked along Genie Street for a door with the tell-tale purple glow. That would show it had been hit by the magic street lamp's light.

Instead she saw a purple blur coming towards her, very fast.

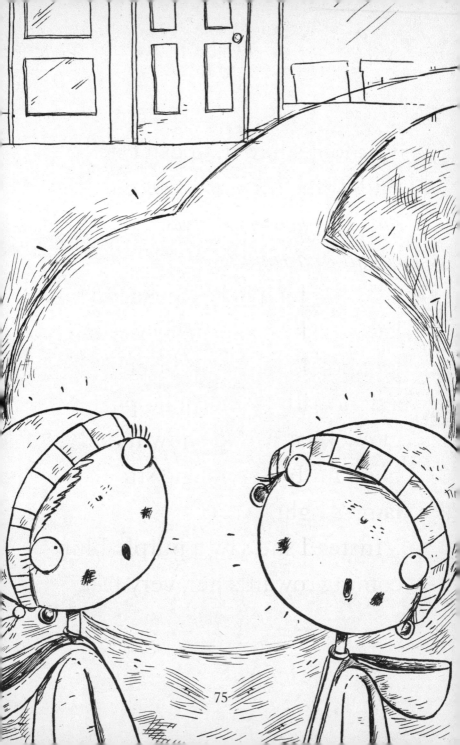

Chapter Two
Madame Who?

'Stand clear, bless my ears!'
Mr Mistry, the Genie Street
postman, was zooming towards
the children on a purple sledge.

'Special Delivereeeeeeeee!'
he cried, as he shot past.

A parcel came flying Tom's
way. He just managed to
catch it.

Mr Mistry vanished as quickly as he had arrived.

'That's funny!' said Daisy, peering at the snow. 'His sledge hasn't left any tracks...' She shook her head, then looked at Tom. 'Who's the parcel for?'

Tom read the label.

'It just says "Madame Zarr",' he said. 'There's no address.'

Daisy looked puzzled.

'I don't know anybody called that. Do you?'

'Nope!' said Tom. 'Perhaps we should ask at the corner shop.'

'Good idea,' agreed Daisy. 'Mr Figby knows everyone.'

Mr Figby and his wife ran Figbys' General Store, on the corner of Genie Street. They had lived in their flat above the shop for many years.

The children made their
way to Figbys'.

'Look!' said Daisy. 'They've
got a new sign!'

The big letters that spelt
out 'FIGBYS' GENERAL
STORE' had been in red paint
before. Now they were purple,
and glowed brightly.

Tom frowned. 'Wait a
minute...'

But Daisy was already
heading through the shop door.

83

Chapter Three
A Surprise in Store

Tom followed Daisy into
Figbys' General Store.

But, somehow, that wasn't
where the door led. Instead,
the children found themselves
overlooking a grassy meadow.
They were standing next
to a set of wooden steps
belonging to a brightly
painted old-fashioned caravan.

More colourful wooden caravans stood nearby. Outside one, a lady was practising juggling. On the steps of another, a man with bright red hair was trying on a huge pair of shoes.

An enormous red-and-white stripy tent was pitched next to the caravans.

'That's a Big Top!' cried Tom. 'We're at the circus!'

'The Lampland Travelling Circus, to be precise,' purred a familiar voice.

Jinx was lazing on the steps. He stretched and yawned.

'Do you recognize where you are?' he asked.

Daisy looked around. 'That's Castle Kinghold!' she cried, pointing. 'We must be in the Rainbow Meadows!'

'Correct,' purred Jinx. 'The circus calls here every year. This year, even the King of Lampland has come to watch. They put on quite a show.' He stretched again, then jumped down from the step. 'Come and see for yourselves.' He padded off towards the Big Top.

Tom followed, but Daisy hesitated.

She could hear someone crying. The sobs were coming from inside the caravan.

Chapter Four
Mrs Figby's Nerves

Daisy knocked gently on the caravan's door. After a few moments, the sobbing stopped. A woman's voice said, 'Come in!'

A lady was sitting at the caravan's dressing table. She was wearing a sparkly leotard and tutu. She looked very upset.

'Mrs Figby!' said Daisy. 'What are you doing here?'

'Hello, Daisy!' said a surprised Mrs Figby. She wiped away a tear. 'You may well ask! I'm supposed to be the star of the show! But it's all going to go horribly wrong, I know it is! And in front of the King of Lampland, too! Oh dear, oh dear!'

'I'm a trapeze artist, here in Lampland,' Mrs Figby told Daisy. 'I've performed my act hundreds of times – but never in front of royalty! I can't do it! I've completely lost my nerve! I'm shaking so much, I'll never be able to keep hold of the trapeze! And there's no safety net, so if I fall…' She shuddered.

Daisy had noticed a poster stuck to Mrs Figby's mirror.

'That's me,' sniffed Mrs Figby.

'"The Amazing Madame Zarr, Queen of the Air",' read Daisy. 'So you're Madame Zarr!'

Mrs Figby nodded. 'That's my stage name. Why?'

'Never mind!' cried Daisy. 'Just come with me, quickly!'

Tom had the Special Delivery parcel. They had to catch up with him.

Chapter Five
Tom in a Spin

Tom had been excited about seeing the circus. But things were not turning out quite as he had expected.

He and Jinx had joined the audience in the Big Top only moments ago. But now, somehow, Tom found himself in the spotlight.

Tom had been plucked from the crowd by two clowns. They had grabbed him by the arms and marched him into the middle of the ring.

Before he knew what was happening, the clowns had taken the parcel out of Tom's hands and put it on the ground. Then they had strapped him to a large, round target.

Now the target was beginning to turn. It slowly sped up. Tom felt a bit sick.

A man in a black top hat
and tailcoat stepped into
the spotlight.

'Your Royal Highness! Ladies
and gentlemen!' shouted the
ringmaster. 'May I present
the one and only Bozo, the
Magnificent!'

Another clown stepped
forward. He was wearing
a blindfold and carrying a
set of throwing knives.

Tom felt even worse.

There was a drum-roll. The
crowd fell silent. Tom shut
his eyes. Then – THUNK!
Something slammed into
the target right next to
Tom's left ear.

THUNK! THUNK!
THUNK-THUNK-THUNK!

One after another, five more
knives narrowly missed him.
The audience went crazy.

Tom felt the target slow down,
then stop. He remembered to
breathe again.

Chapter Six
The Queen of the Air

Tom enjoyed the applause
a lot more than the act. He
took several bows. Suddenly,
Daisy burst into the ring.
There was a lady in a sparkly
circus costume with her.

'Mrs… Figby?' said Tom.
He still felt a bit dizzy. 'Is
that you?'

'Yes! But she's Madame Zarr, too!' cried Daisy impatiently. 'Have you still got Mr Mistry's Special Delivery?'

Tom quickly picked up the parcel from beside the target. He gave it to Mrs Figby.

'For me? Thank you, dear!' said Mrs Figby. She tried to smile but her stage fright was getting worse. The children could see her hands trembling as she unwrapped the parcel.

'How lovely!' gasped Mrs Figby. 'But why do I need this, dear?'

Inside the parcel was a sparkly tiara. It had three silver feathers on it.

'Try it on, Mrs Figby!' urged Daisy.

Mrs Figby tried it on. She immediately stopped trembling. Her face lit up with delight.

'Why, I feel altogether different!' she beamed. 'As if I could float on air. I believe I could do *anything*!'

'And now, ladies and gentlemen, for our next act!' bellowed the ringmaster.

Tom had just realized something. 'Daisy!' he whispered. 'The ringmaster! It's Mr Figby!'

'It is my great pleasure,' Mr Figby went on, 'to introduce the beautiful, the magnificent, the amazing Madame Zarr, Queen of the Air!' He glanced across at his wife. 'You're on, dear!' he hissed.

Mrs Figby's act was a triumph. In her feather tiara, she was completely fearless. She gave the most daring and dazzling performance of her life. High above, she flipped and twirled between trapezes as if she could fly. Tom and Daisy gasped and cheered with the rest of the crowd.

When it was over, the king led a standing ovation.

Chapter Seven
Happy Landings

'The time has come,' Mr Figby announced, 'for the Grand Finale of our show!'

'This should be good!' whispered Tom.

'Ladies and gentlemen, I give you,' bellowed Mr Figby, 'the one-and-only brother-and-sister human-cannonball act – Tom and Daisy!'

Tom's smile vanished. Several clown helpers came rushing over. They fitted Tom and Daisy with crash helmets and bundled them over to a large cannon. Before they knew it, the children found themselves loaded inside.

There was another drum-roll. Tom and Daisy looked at one another with wide eyes.

'Happy landings!' cried Mr Figby. He lit the cannon's fuse.

Tom and Daisy listened
to the fizzle of the fuse,
hearts pounding…

BOOOOOM!

The children shot into the
air. They rocketed through
the canvas roof of the Big Top
and out into the open sky.
Then they began to fall.
The ground came racing up
horribly fast. They closed
their eyes, expecting to be
squashed flat…

THWUMP!

The children landed in
something soft, wet and cold.
They were lying in a snowdrift,
outside Figbys' General Store.

Daisy got up and brushed
herself off. Two red clown noses
lay in the snow by her feet.
Daisy tried one on. Her hair
turned bright red.

'Great souvenirs!' laughed
Tom. 'Who *nose* when they'll
come in handy?'

Daisy groaned. A joke as bad as
that deserved a giant snowball…

GENIE STREET

Fan Pages

Here's what other children have to say about Genie Street and their favourite Lampland characters!

'I loved reading this book, it was very funny and it made me laugh. It was great to have a story about gladiators as I'm learning about them at school.' Alicia, age 7

'It was so exciting! I loved the fierce lions, dungeons and gladiators.' Freddy, age 6

'I loved Madame Zarr, Circus Star, because I could read it myself with Mummy. I want a magic lamp on our street so I can go on adventures and see our neighbours do funny things, too.' Vincent, age 6

'My favourite character was Tom because he jokes around a lot.' Hannah, age 7

'I loved this book. The magic and adventures were great. Can I read some more?!' Meredith, age 7

Genie Street is a brand-new fiction series that
is the next step up from Ladybird's Read it yourself
Level 4. Ideal for newly independent Key Stage 1
readers, these books are for children who want
to read real fiction for the first time.

Collect all the titles in the series:

9781409312390

9781409312406

9781409312413

9781409312420

9781409312437

9781409312444

Each book contains two easy-to-read stories
that children will love. The stories include short
chapters, simple vocabulary and a clear layout
that will encourage and build confidence when reading.